# LET'S DANCE, GRANDMA!

For Audrey, the grandma who loves to dance

Let's Dance, Grandma!

Copyright © 2014 by Nigel McMullen

All rights reserved. Manufactured in China.

No part of this book may be used or reproduced in any manner whatsoever without written permission except in the case of brief quotations embodied in critical articles and reviews. For information address HarperCollins Children's Books, a division of HarperCollins Publishers, 10 East 53rd Street, New York, NY 10022.

www.harpercollinschildrens.com

Library of Congress Cataloging-in-Publication Data is available.

ISBN 978-0-06-050747-3

The artist used watercolors to create the illustrations for this book.

Typography by Jeanne L. Hogle

13  14  15  16  17   SCP   10  9  8  7  6  5  4  3  2  1

❖

First Edition

# LET'S DANCE, GRANDMA!

### Nigel McMullen

**HARPER**
*An Imprint of HarperCollinsPublishers*

More than anything,
Lucy loved to dance.

But whenever Grandma came to visit, Mom said, "No dancing, Lucy. You'll wear Grandma out. Grandmas don't dance."

But this time Lucy couldn't help herself. The first thing she said when Mom had gone was,

"Dance, Grandma, dance?"

But Grandma shook her head, and they
played ball instead.

Lucy soon got bored with that and asked again,

"Dance, Grandma, dance?"

But Grandma shook her head, so Lucy pretended
Grandma was a horse and rode around on her back.

Grandma said her back was aching, so they played dress-up instead.

Lucy pretended to be a lion
and roared at Grandma.

After dress-up, they played cards.

Grandma asked if Lucy would like a book to read while she had a rest.

But Lucy decided to try again.

"Dance, Grandma, dance?"

Grandma shook her head and said, "No, but let's play hide-and-seek instead." And off she went to hide.

Poor Grandma, thought Lucy. Mom was right.
Grandmas don't dance.

"Cuddle, Grandma,
cuddle?"

Lucy asked softly.

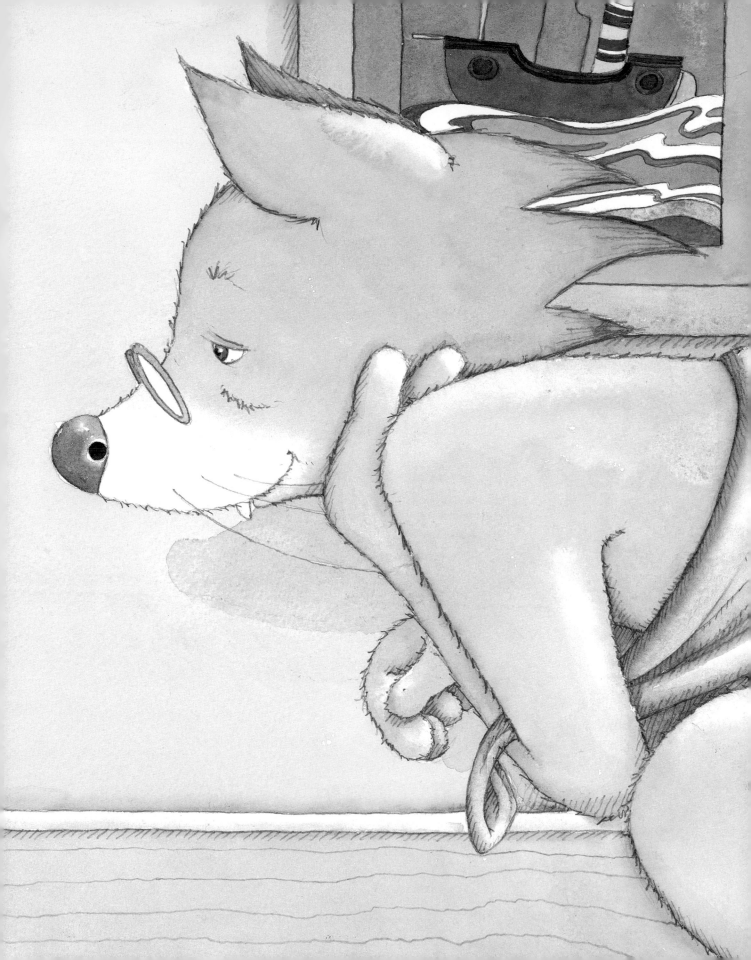

Grandma smiled, picked Lucy up, and began to sing a lullaby. It was the same lullaby she'd sung to Lucy's mom when she was little.

And as Grandma sang, she swayed . . . and as she swayed, she began to dance . . . slowly at first, but then faster, until it seemed to Lucy that the whole world was dancing.

"We're dancing, we're dancing!"

she said.

"Yes," said Grandma.

"But I thought grandmas don't dance," said Lucy.

"Oh, they do," said Grandma,
"but only with very special people."